Average JOE

published by

National Center for Youth Issues
Practical Guidance Resources Educators Can Trust
ncyi.org

'JAKE' 'ANGUS' 'KIRBY'

To Claire
Never settle for average.

Duplication and Copyright

No part of this publication may be reproduced, stored in a retrieval system or transmitted in any form by any means, electronic, mechanical, photocopy, recording or otherwise without prior written permission from the publisher except for all worksheets and activities which may be reproduced for a specific group or class. Reproduction for an entire school or school district is prohibited.

Average Joe

ISBN: 978-1-937870-00-3
Written by: Julia Cook
Cover Design and Illustrations by: Anita DuFalla
Interior Design by: Phillip W. Rodgers
Published by National Center for Youth Issues
First Edition • Softcover

© 2011 National Center for Youth Issues, Chattanooga, TN
All rights reserved.

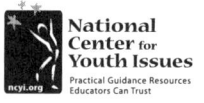

P.O. Box 22185
Chattanooga, TN 37422-2185
423.899.5714 • 800.477.8277
fax: 423.899.4547
www.ncyi.org

Printed at RR Donnelley
Crawfordsville, Indiana, USA
November 2011

CONTENTS

CHAPTER ONE	**Another Long Year**	5
CHAPTER TWO	**Cody Annoying**	9
CHAPTER THREE	**Too Much Homework!**	12
CHAPTER FOUR	**Flawless Forever**	15
CHAPTER FIVE	**Close Call!**	18
CHAPTER SIX	**Bim the Bully**	21
CHAPTER SEVEN	**Termination Experiment**	24
CHAPTER EIGHT	**Perfect Timing**	27
CHAPTER NINE	**Idiot Bim Bum**	29
CHAPTER TEN	**Two for One**	32
CHAPTER ELEVEN	**Strategic Planning**	36
CHAPTER TWELVE	**Teacher Talk**	38
CHAPTER THIRTEEN	**It's Pay Back Time!**	42
CHAPTER FOURTEEN	**No More Worries**	46
CHAPTER FIFTEEN	**How Will He Know Us?**	49
CHAPTER SIXTEEN	**Another Close Call!**	51
CHAPTER SEVENTEEN	**Karma**	56
CHAPTER EIGHTEEN	**Love Note**	59
CHAPTER NINETEEN	**Termination of the Homework Ogre**	63
CHAPTER TWENTY	**Special Delivery**	67
CHAPTER TWENTY-ONE	**Fashion Police Needed!**	69
CHAPTER TWENTY-TWO	**Bim on Steroids**	72
CHAPTER TWENTY-THREE	**Business as Usual**	76
CHAPTER TWENTY-FOUR	**It Worked!**	78
CHAPTER TWENTY-FIVE	**The BIG Date**	80
CHAPTER TWENTY-SIX	**Not-So-Average Joe after All**	85

FOR LUCAS!

CHAPTER ONE
Another Long Year

My name is Joe. I am a 12-year old stuck inside a nine-year old's body FOREVER!

Three years ago, my dad, the brilliant scientist, was working on his latest invention: a top secret anti-aging serum.

The whole idea behind the serum was to slow down the aging process in grown-ups.

It worked great on my mom...and it's still working today...she looks a lot younger than most moms.

One night, just as I was heading to bed, I overheard my parents talking. "This stuff is so amazing," my mom said to my dad. "I look and feel so young! What do you think would happen if you gave your serum to a child? Do you think it would turn them into an infant?"

"Well, often medicine has the opposite effect on children," my dad told her. "Since the serum reversed the aging process and made you younger, I think there is a high probability that it would make a child appear older. That child might even transform into an adult."

How cool would that be! I thought to myself. *I would love to be a grown-up.*

Later that night while my parents were asleep, I went down into our basement. I sneaked into my dad's lab, and took some of the top secret anti-aging serum.

Within a few seconds, I exploded into a 22-year old man. I even had facial hair!

I ran upstairs to my parents' bedroom and woke them up. I will never forget the look on their faces: scared, mad, guilty, and sad all at the same time.

My dad was convinced that he had ruined my life.

Luckily, two hours later, the serum wore off and I changed back into my regular nine-year old self. But the serum had one side effect. I stopped growing.

AVERAGE JOE

I never grow...I never change -unless I drink the secret serum and become 22 for two hours. Like I said... I am a 12-year old stuck inside a nine-year old's body FOREVER!

People started asking questions because everyone around me was changing and growing, and I was staying exactly the same. At first, we got away with telling them that I was just a late bloomer, but after a while, our neighbors and friends started getting suspicious.

My dad is working hard on a new formula so that he can fix me, but until he figures it out, we have to keep moving around from town to town and school to school.

This is my third school in three years and here I sit in my fourth grade class for the third time...being "Average Joe".

Dad says that it is very important that I don't stand out. He wants me to be the average kid that nobody really notices. He wants me to just fade in with everybody else. The truth is, I am totally bored! It's bad enough that I have to be in the fourth grade for one year let alone three!!! And, since I just moved again, I have no friends...as in zero...I don't think anyone even notices that I am here.

My teacher's name is Miss Finkelstein. It almost sounds like Miss Frankenstein, but she certainly doesn't look like Frankenstein. In fact, she's actually kinda cute...Not that I would ever admit that to anyone.

"Good morning class! My name is Miss Finkelstein, and I am so excited to be your teacher! I just graduated from college, and this will be my very first year of teaching. We are going to make a great team!"

Great, I thought to myself... Not only do I have be in the fourth grade for the third time, I have to break in a brand new teacher!

It's going to be another very long year!

CHAPTER TWO
Cody Annoying

School's been in session for about three weeks now, but this year is a lot different from my other fourth grade years. Miss Finkelstein gives more homework than both of my other fourth grade teachers put together! The only thing that hasn't changed are the spelling words. They are exactly the same as they were last year...and the year before. That makes it really nice for me because I never have to study. I always miss four or five words on the pre- test so that Miss Finkelstein won't think I'm smart and give me the gifted list. The gifted list has words on it like "jurisprudence" and "kinesiology"- words that nobody ever uses, so why should I have to learn how to spell them?

I know I'm supposed to just fit in and not be noticed, but it's really hard to act like I'm nine when I am really 12. Nine-year-olds make up their own rules on the soccer field - probably because they don't know the real rules.

And, they tattle! Now I've known some tattlers in the last three years, but nobody tattles like Cody Annoying. His actual name is Cody Anderson, but I call him "Cody Annoying" - because HE IS!!!

Yesterday, Miss Finkelstein gave each of us three pieces of lined paper and a piece of construction paper. She asked us to write a story about something that we had done over the summer and then design a cover for our story. She told us to write the story and then draw the cover, but since I can draw a lot better than I can write, I wanted to make my cover first and then write about what I had drawn.

I grabbed my construction paper and started to draw a picture of the moving van that moved all of our stuff this summer. The guy who drove the moving van was really nice. He let me sit in the cab of the semi and showed me how to move the hydraulic lift! I couldn't believe how many dials and knobs there were on the dashboard. I felt like I was a pilot sitting in a cockpit of a fighter plane. It was awesome!

Just as I had finished the outline of the semi, I heard Cody Annoying's squeaky little voice: "Teacher, Joe's doing his cover first."

AVERAGE JOE

Why did Cody care? What business of his was it that I wanted to draw my cover before I wrote my story?

"Joe," Miss Finkelstein said. "The instructions are that you need to write your story and then draw."

"But I am so much better at dra...."

"Joe! Follow the instructions!" she said.

Rats! I thought to myself. *Now I have to draw the picture in my head, write about it, and then draw it again on the paper.*

I looked over at Cody Annoying and shot him a mean dart with my eyes. He wouldn't look at me. He just sat in his seat smiling and pretending to write.

This school year just keeps getting longer!

CHAPTER THREE
Too Much Homework!

I can't believe how much homework Miss Finkelstein gives! Tonight, I have two pages of math, my summer story to finish, spelling sentences, and three sections of boring social studies to read with questions to answer. And to top it all off, my favorite show, *Adventures of Slime Man*, is on TV! Fourth grade has never been this hard! I seriously think that Miss Finkelstein doesn't want us to have a life outside of school.

At least I don't have to go to karate tonight after school like Marvin does. He's going to have to stay up all night again to get all of his homework done.

AVERAGE JOE

Marvin is the first friend that I made this year. He's probably one of the best friends I have ever had. Most kids would just say "forget it" and just go to bed if they had too much homework. But not "Marvin the Academic Maniac"!!! He has to get A's on everything or he'll explode!

I walked into my house just as my mom was laying out my dress-up clothes. I don't dress up very often and since I don't grow, I have had the same dress-up clothes for three years.

"What are those for?" I asked.

"Joe, you remember, tonight is Turtle's accordion recital, and we're all going as a family."

Turtle is my little sister. Her real name is Alexandra, but my mom nicknamed her "Turtle" because she wants her to slow down. My dad says that Turtle is the only person he knows who can be in seven rooms at once! She is super hyper and is constantly moving and talking...unless she's asleep.

"But, Mom, I can't go! I have way too much homework and besides, my show is on tonight."

"Joe! Turtle's accordion recital is much more important than watching your show! Let me see how much homework you have."

I pulled out all of my stuff and showed it to my mom.

"Well," she said, "Turtle is important, but your grades are more important than her recital. I don't see how you can get all of this done tonight and be in bed by nine if you go with us. But don't count on watching your show tonight because you won't have time to do that either. What kind of a teacher gives that much homework to a fourth grader anyway? At least you should know the material by now."

"Not really," I said. "The only thing that hasn't changed since last year and the year before are my spelling words, and I still have to do sentences."

Turtle used to be five years younger than me, but now she is seven and I am stuck at nine. If my dad doesn't figure out a way to fix me, Turtle is going to become my big sister. She'll start to think that she's the boss of me and that will be a total disaster!!!

That's it! I thought to myself, *I'll just drink the secret serum and become 22 for a few hours. When I'm 22, I'll be able to do my homework super fast and still have time to watch Slime Man! Since Turtle's accordion recital will last for at least two hours plus drive time, I'll have plenty of time to get everything done and switch back into me before they get home.*

CHAPTER FOUR
Flawless Forever

My dad keeps an ongoing supply of his secret serum under lock and key in the back closet of his lab. Luckily, I know where he keeps a spare key. He made the extra key for my mom in case he is out of town when she needs to take her monthly dose. She has it taped to the back of her underwear drawer.

My dad calls the serum "Flawless Forever". When he first invented it, he was certain that he'd come up with a miracle drug. That is until he gave it to me. I found a flaw.

Dad would never approve of me taking Flawless Forever without him being there with me. I've only taken it four times in the last three years. I always take it in the lab when I'm hooked up to all of my dad's special gizmos and machines so he can monitor me closely. To get back to normal, Dad says he has to invent the perfect "switch back serum" (SBS for short) for me to take during the two-hour time frame when I am 22. So far, he's tried out four different versions of SBS. Unfortunately, none of them have had any effect at all.

I found the key right where I knew it would be. I pulled the tape from the drawer, peeled it off of the key, grabbed a glass from the kitchen, and headed for my dad's lab in the basement. I opened up the door of the lab and started walking toward the back closet. LOCKED!!! The closet was locked! I took a chance and tried the key that opened the lab door. No such luck...

If I were my dad, where would I put the key to the closet? I grabbed a stool and pushed it up in front of the door. I climbed up on the stool and slid my hand along the top of the door frame. Found it!

I spotted the Flawless Forever as soon as I opened the door. My dad kept the purple-colored liquid in a five-gallon container on the middle shelf. The container had a spigot at the bottom of it. I grabbed my glass and lined it up with the spigot. Since the dosage for a kid my size was only a teaspoon, nobody would even notice that I had taken some. I poured a tiny bit of Flawless Forever into the bottom of the glass and put the spigot back exactly the way it was. I locked the closet door, put the key on the top of the door frame, and put the stool away.

I locked the lab door and ran upstairs. Putting the key back in my mom's underwear drawer was tricky because I couldn't get the tape to stick. I ran to my dad's office and got a new piece of tape. PERFECT! Now the fun begins!

CHAPTER FIVE
Close Call!

I went to the kitchen and grabbed my mom's measuring spoons and headed for my bedroom. Getting the teaspoon full and into my mouth without spilling was tough. It was much easier to take the right dose when my dad was giving it to me.

As soon as the Flawless Forever hit my tongue, I remembered how nasty it tasted. It was super bitter, majorly sour, and just plain nasty! How can my mom stand to take this every month? GAG! GAG! GAG! YUK!!!!!

AVERAGE JOE

The minute I swallowed, my throat began to itch, my eyes started to water and within seconds, I exploded into a grown-up!

Rats! I split my brand new school jeans into shreds! My shirt stretched out into a muscle shirt. In the mirror, I looked like a body builder wearing a grass skirt! My mom's gonna kill me!!! I should have remembered to put on my dad's clothes before I swallowed the secret serum.

I ran to my dad's room and grabbed a pair of sweats and put them on. Then, I stuffed my shredded pants into the front pocket of my backpack. My mom never looks in my backpack. I'll just throw my pants away at school tomorrow. If I'm lucky, she'll forget about those pants, and she'll never know.

I got through my math in ten minutes. I even did the super hard extra credit problem. It didn't seem very hard at all! My spelling sentences only took me five minutes, and I read all three sections of my social studies and answered the questions in less than 15 minutes. I used the rest of the first hour to finish my summer story, and I made it sound awesome.

I couldn't believe how fast I got my homework done! I felt like a genius! Everything came so easy! I hope Miss Finkelstein doesn't think that my mom wrote my summer story for me.

Slime Man came on at eight o'clock, and I got to watch the entire episode uninterrupted. Turtle wasn't there to constantly talk and continually ask questions about what was going on. What a totally amazing night! I got all of my homework done, I got to watch my show without being interrupted, AND I got out of going to Turtle's accordion recital!

"*So much for being* "AVERAGE JOE" *tonight*," I thought to myself.

Just as my parents were pulling into the driveway, the Flawless Forever wore off, and I shrunk back into my normal nine-year old self. Shrinking doesn't hurt. In fact, it kinda tickles.

"Joe, you missed a great recital!" my mom said. "Turtle was fantastic! Did you get all of your homework done?"

"Yep, I even did the extra credit!" I said.

"Why are you wearing your dad's sweats?" my mom asked. "They are way too big for you!"

"Ummm, I like my sweats baggy," I said. And then I went to bed.

CHAPTER SIX
Bim the Bully

Today, as soon as I got to school, Bim came right up to my face. "Hey, Joe," he said. "I need to copy your math."

Bim is the class bully. Size wise, he's the opposite of me. He is nine and looks like he's 12, and I'm a 12-year old who looks nine! Bim thinks he's the coolest person on the planet. He also thinks that everybody likes him. Actually, the kids just pretend to like him because they are all scared of him. Personally, I think Bim is an idiot! First of all, who would name their kid Bim? It sounds like Bum! If I was 12 on the outside, I'd kick Bim's bum and knock some sense into him!

There was no way I was going to let Bim Bum copy my math. I knew I had all of my problems right, and I even got the super hard extra credit one done. Miss Finkelstein would know that Bim had copied because he always misses at least five problems in math. What happens is, everybody always does what Bim tells them to do because if you don't, he'll haul off and punch you in the face.

"Uh sorry, Bim, I don't have my math with me," I said. "I accidentally left it on the kitchen table this morning, and my mom's going to bring it over and drop it off in the office on her way to work."

I squinted up my face and braced myself to take a punch......

"Oh, that's okay, Joe. I'll just catch you next time," he said.

I watched Bim head straight for Marvin. Marvin the Academic Maniac actually started taking karate because of Bim. Bim always copies off of Marvin, and from what other kids tell me, it's been going on since kindergarten.

Marvin told me last week that his life-long goal is to know karate well enough to stand up to Bim without getting beat up. Right now, he only has an orange belt, and he says he'll need at least a brown.

AVERAGE JOE

I watched Marvin squint, crouch down, and slowly hand over his math to Bim. I mean Bim Bum!

Marvin is scared to death of Bim. The rumor is that in kindergarten, Bim scared Marvin so bad that he peed his pants at school. I don't think Marvin has ever gotten over it.

Just before math class, I used the hall pass and made it look like I was going to the office to get my homework. I went to my locker and grabbed my math paper, and then killed some time in the boy's bathroom. Bim never suspected anything.

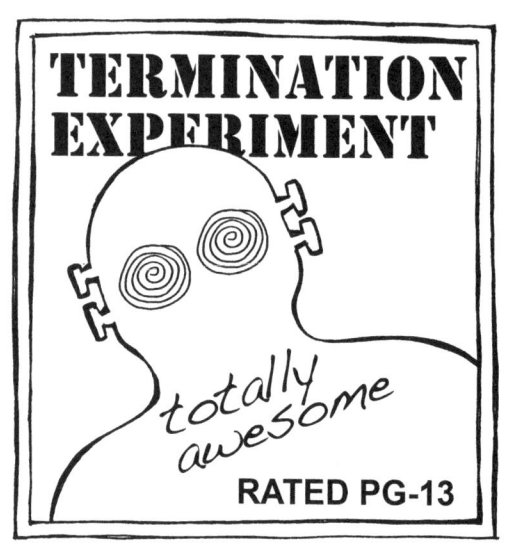

CHAPTER SEVEN
Termination Experiment

This afternoon out at recess, Marvin and my other best friend Jack were talking about the new movie *Termination Experiment*. "I would give anything to see that movie," Marvin said.

"Yeah, me too," said Jack. "But since it's PG-13 my parents won't let me see it, and there's no way the theater people will let you in if you're not with a grown-up."

As soon as I heard the word "grown-up", something clicked inside my head, and before I could stop myself, I blurted out the most amazing idea ever!

"I've seen it," I said.

"Yeah right," said Jack. "Your mom would never let you go see a PG-13 movie, especially that one."

"She doesn't know about it. My Uncle Joe took me to see it last Saturday. It was awesome!"

"I didn't know you had an Uncle Joe," Marvin said.

"He's my dad's little brother. He's been away at college, but he just moved in with us. Now he's going to go to college here. I'm named after him, and I look a lot like him too."

"Would your Uncle Joe take us to see *Termination Experiment?*" Jack asked.

"I'm sure he would, but you'd probably have to pay his way in plus another ten bucks. My mom says he's a struggling college student with very little money and very little time."

"That's a lot of money," said Marvin. "But, if all three of us go in together, it won't be that bad."

"I'd pay a million dollars to see it on the big screen," Jack said. "Do you think he can go this Saturday?"

"He probably can, but I can't. I have to go to dinner at my other grandma's house."

"Rats!" said Marvin. "That means we're going to have to split it two ways. That will take my entire month's allowance."

"Yeah, but Marvin, it's *Termination Experiment!*" Jack said. "It will be so worth it!"

"It is one of the best movies I have ever seen. . .," I said.

"OK, OK," said Marvin. "See if your Uncle Joe can go to the one o'clock show on Saturday."

"I'll ask him, and I'll let you know tomorrow."

As soon as I got home from school, I asked my mom if I could go to the show on Saturday with Jack and Marvin.

"What show?" my mom asked. "I certainly don't want you to go see that *Termination Experiment* movie. The critics say that it's way too violent for kids."

"Oh," I said. "We can't even go to that one unless we are with a grown-up because it's PG-13. We want to go see the new *Slime Man* movie again."

"Joe, you've already seen that show three times! Aren't you sick of it yet?"

"I could never get sick of *Slime Man*, Mom."

"Well, OK, but you'll have to go to the one o'clock show because we have dinner at Grandma's that night."

Perfect! I thought to myself. *This just might work!*

CHAPTER EIGHT
Perfect Timing

With only four days until Saturday, I have a lot of work to do if I want to pull this off. First of all, I need to figure out how to get my hands on some Flawless Forever without my parents finding out.

I have to find a time when I am home alone - which doesn't exactly happen very often. On Thursdays, Mom takes Turtle to her ping pong lessons at five. Turtle's main goal in life this week is to someday become Ping Pong Champion of the World! I seriously think my parents sign Turtle up for everything they can just to keep her from driving everyone else nuts.

My dad goes running for about an hour as soon as he gets home from work every day, but the problem is, I never know when he will be home. Sometimes he's home by five, but if he's working on a lab project and it takes longer than it should, he doesn't get home until six or seven.

If my dad doesn't have to work late on Thursday, I'll be alone in the house for at least a half hour. That's plenty of time to sneak into the lab.

That night, I asked my dad if he could be home by 6:30 to watch our favorite TV show, *Robotic International*.

"I thought that show was on Friday night," he said.

"It usually is," I told him. "But the season premiere is on this Thursday."

"Well, I think that should work," Dad said. "As long as I can get my run in first."

PERFECT, I thought to myself. *This may end up being easier than I thought it would be. Now, if I can just make it through the next three days!*

CHAPTER NINE
Idiot Bim Bum

Tuesday and Wednesday seemed to crawl by. Two days felt more like two weeks. All I could think about was how much fun I was going to have at *Termination Experiment*!!! It seemed like Saturday was never going to get here.

On Thursday, Marvin brought his movie money to school. He wanted to pay me in advance so my Uncle Joe wouldn't back out (like that would ever happen!)

Marvin told me to meet him on the corner across from the playground after school so he could give me his money.

"Why don't you just pay me now?" I asked.

"Because I want to show Jack. Besides, I love having this much money on me!"

Marvin showed his money to Jack at recess. Unfortunately, Cody Annoying saw the money too, and overheard Marvin talking about his plan.

After recess, Cody went straight to Miss Finkelstein and said, "Marvin has a whole bunch of money in his pocket and he's going to give it to Joe on the corner after school so Joe's uncle will take him to a movie and we aren't supposed to bring money to school because it says so in the school handbook."

Fortunately, Miss Finkelstein is so sick of Cody telling on everyone, that sometimes she tunes him out. She was in the middle of answering a text message on her phone when Cody started talking, so I think she only heard about a fourth of what he said.

Unfortunately, Bim heard the whole thing.

Leave it to Bim Bum to show his true idiot colors. Just as Marvin was handing over his money to me at the corner after school, Bim showed up.

"Hey Marv," Bim called out. (Marvin HATES being called "Marv"). "What's the money for?"

"Nothing," Marvin said.

AVERAGE JOE

"Well if it's for nothing, then you should be paying me so that I don't break your face! Hand it over NOW!"

"Hey Bim," I said. "Back OFF!"

"Stay out of this Joe, or I'll have to mess your face up too!"

Marvin started to squirm. He looked like he had just bitten into a dog poo sandwich. His face turned sheet white and he started to sweat.

Tears streamed down Marvin's cheeks as he handed his movie money, and an entire month's allowance, over to Bim.

"I should just hit you anyway just to toughen you up, you big baby! Are you going to pee your pants now, Marv?" he asked as he tucked Marvin's money into his back pocket.

Bim smiled like he had just aced a math test, and then turned and walked away. Marvin hid his face from me so I couldn't see him cry. As soon as Bim was out of sight, Marvin stood up. He tried to talk to me but when he opened his mouth, nothing came out and his eyes started to water again. Then Marvin turned around and ran toward his house.

If I was bigger than Bim, I'd pick him up by his hair! I thought to myself...

And then, I got another fantastic idea!

CHAPTER TEN
Two for One

My mom and Turtle left for Ping Pong at 4:45 - right on schedule. Ten minutes later, my dad got home. *Perfect!* I thought to myself. *I'll have plenty of time!*

Just as my dad was walking out the door to go running, his phone rang. *Oh no! What if it's my Uncle Gary?* I thought. My dad always talks to him <u>forever</u>. If it's Gary, he'll be on the phone for at least an hour. Then my mom will be back before he leaves to go running, and I won't be able to sneak into the...

"OK", my dad said. "Just give me a call if it doesn't work out. I'm leaving for a run right now, but I'll be back in an hour and I'm home all night."

AVERAGE JOE

Whew! What a relief! I thought.

As my dad hung up the phone, he shook his head. "I don't think the guys at my work lab can tie their own shoes by themselves unless I'm there to tell them how to do it," he said. "Get your homework done so we can watch *Robotics* when I get back."

As soon as my dad rounded the corner, I ran to my mom's underwear drawer to grab the key. I couldn't get Marvin's face out of my head. I had to get Marvin's money back from Bim. Time for Bim Bum to get a dose of his own medicine.

I ran into the kitchen and looked under the sink for a container to put the Flawless Forever in. I needed something with a lid, because this time, I needed two doses.

Tucked way in the back of the cupboard behind the cutting board, I saw the perfect container. Last year at the county fair, my mom bought us a jug of homemade root beer. It was the best root beer I had ever tasted! A man filled the jug from a big wooden barrel and then sealed it shut with a rubber stopper that was attached.

"Save this jug," he said. "Then next year, bring it back and I'll refill it for half price."

Good thing my mom saved it because it was exactly what I was looking for.

I headed downstairs, and opened up the lab. It seemed like it was a lot easier to get into this time. I lined up the spigot with the bottle and pulled the lever back. I only needed two doses (about two teaspoons,) but when I went to push the lever back, it got stuck and a ton of Flawless Forever came out into the root beer bottle.

I tried to figure out how to open the top of the tank so that I could pour some of the serum back in, but there was a hose, a big dial, and some clamps on the top of the tank and I couldn't figure out how to open it.

Oh well, I thought to myself. *I can always pour what I don't need down the sink.*

I locked the lab, put both keys back where they belong, and headed to my bedroom. I stashed the Flawless Forever in the back of my closet and covered it with dirty clothes.

My mom always gets mad at me when I don't put my dirty clothes in the hamper. It just works better for me to throw them in the bottom of my closet.

I ran into my parent's bedroom and grabbed a pair of my dad's tennis shoes, sweats, and a t-shirt and stuffed them into my backpack.

Then, I went and sat down at the kitchen table to start my homework.

AVERAGE JOE

Miss Finkelstein is ridiculous! Tonight, I have three pages of math to do, 25 spelling sentences to write, five sections of social studies to read and answer questions for, and I have to go outside and find a place in our yard where erosion has taken place and then write a paragraph about what I see.

I wish I had time to take Flawless Forever tonight. I'll never get done in time to watch *Robotics International* with my dad.

CHAPTER. ELEVEN
Strategic Planning

By the time my mom got home with Turtle, the only homework I had finished was my erosion paragraph.

"Mom," I said. "I have to go to school early tomorrow."

"Why?" she asked.

"Because we're having a planning meeting for the school play, and I want to be on the set design committee, so we have to meet and talk about what we are going to make."

"Well," she said. "I have water aerobics at 7 a.m. Turtle is going with me to the gym because I'm enrolling her in a before school 'Pilates for Peanuts' class. I won't be home, but Dad will be here."

"Be where?" my dad asked as he came through the door.

"Be here with Joe tomorrow morning, he has to go into school early, and Turtle and I will be at the gym." she said.

"I have to be at the lab by six tomorrow," my dad said.

"Well, I could have Grandma come..."

"What? MOM! I'm 12! I don't need Grandma to come over!"

"Well, I'm not so sure. I don't have a problem leaving you alone a little bit in the afternoon, but getting yourself up on time can be tricky. What time do you need to be there?"

"7:15," I said.

"OK then, I will just wake you up before I leave at 6:40. Make sure you eat breakfast and remember to wash your face and remember to brush your..."

"Mom! I'm 12!"

I worked really hard to get my homework done before *Robotics* came on, but I didn't get it finished... no thanks to Miss Finkelstein. Luckily, my dad recorded it. By the time I got to bed, it was 10:45 p.m.

CHAPTER TWELVE
Teacher Talk

I didn't sleep much at all last night because I kept thinking about what I (aka Uncle Joe) was going to say to Bim. I was up and dressed by six, but I hid under my covers and pretended to be asleep until my mom came in to wake me up at 6:35.

The minute she and Turtle left the house, I ran to my closet and grabbed the jug of Flawless Forever.

I might as well change here since nobody's home, I thought to myself. *Besides, I need to take the serum before seven so I can make sure that I'm back to normal by the time school starts at 9:05.*

I grabbed my dad's clothes out of my backpack and changed into them. I put my clothes into my backpack and then headed to the kitchen to get the measuring spoon.

YUK! Ewwww! BLAH!!!! That stuff tasted so bad! Before I could blink, I was huge again! I went to put on my dad's shoes, but they were way too small for my feet. *That's a great sign*, I thought to myself. *When I grow up, I'm going to be bigger than my dad!*

I ran to the garage and grabbed a pair of my dad's flip flops. My heel stuck out over the end, but they were better than nothing. I put the Flawless Forever in the back of my closet and headed for the kitchen.

I poured myself a bowl of cereal just like always, but when I had finished eating it, I was still hungry. I ended up eating three more bowls before I finally headed out the door.

By the time I got to school, it was only 7:30. I knew Bim wouldn't show up until about eight so I just sat on the bench by the bus stop and checked over my homework. I figured I'd start heading down the street toward Bim's house at about 7:50. There was no way I could get away with scaring Bim on the school grounds. I'd get arrested for child abuse!

At 7:35, I saw Miss Finkelstein pull into the parking lot and without thinking, I waved at her. She parked her car and came walking over to me.

"Hi, she said. "Do I know you?"

I froze! My whole body felt like I was trapped inside of an ice cube! *What should I say?* I thought to myself.

"Um…, I'm Joe's uncle," I blurted out.

"Oh! Yes, I should have known! You look just like him! But what are you doing here?" she asked.

"Uhhh, well, I just transferred here to go to college and I'm living with Joe and his family."

"No, what are you doing here at school?"

"Oh, um, Joe's mom had a class at the gym and his dad had to go into work early, so I told them that I'd get him to school. He asked me to check his homework for him, so that's what I'm doing." I said.

"Where is Joe?" she asked.

"He had to use the restroom," I said.

"Oh, well, I'm Jane… Jane Finkelstein. I'm Joe's teacher. It's nice to meet you," she said as she reached out to shake my hand.

"By the way," she asked, "what's your name?"

"I'm Joe," I said.

"Just like your nephew?" she asked.

"Yep, he's named after me," I said proudly.

"Well," Miss Finkelstein said, "maybe I'll see you around, Joe." She smiled at me in a weird way, and then turned around and walked up the sidewalk. Just before she went into the building, she looked back at me, smiled and waved.

Wow! I thought to myself, *my plan for Bim just might work!*

CHAPTER THIRTEEN
It's Pay Back Time!

As soon as Miss Finkelstein was out of sight, I looked down at my watch. It was killing my wrist and the band was just about to rip apart. 7:50 - time to kick Bim's bum! I took my watch off and stuck it in my backpack, and then started walking down the sidewalk toward Bim's house.

After about ten minutes, I spotted Bim heading towards me. My whole body tensed up. I felt like I had swallowed a porcupine! But then, I figured if I could fool Miss Finkelstein, Bim would be a snap.

"Bim!" I yelled out as I got closer to him. "Hey Bim, come over here!"

"Who are you?" Bim asked.

"I'm Joe's uncle, and I need to talk to you about something," I said.

Inside my head, I was doing 40 jumping jacks per second, but on the outside, I amazingly managed to control myself. "Joe told me that you took Marvin's money yesterday, and I'm here to get it back."

"I have no idea what you are talking about," Bim said with a smirk on his face.

I walked right up to Bim, grabbed him by the hair, and pushed him up against the fence. I held him up by his hair until he was standing on his tip toes.

"You're a bully, Bim! You push kids around. You make kids feel scared. You steal homework so you don't have to do it yourself. You're a jerk!"

Bim's face turned as white as a sheet. His eyes got so big that I thought they were going to pop right out of his head.

"You have picked on Marvin since kindergarten!" I said as I pulled harder on his hair. "Yesterday, you took Marvin's money... GIVE IT BACK TO ME NOW!"

"OK, OK, Bim said as his trembling hand reached into his back pocket. "Here it is! Please, let go of my hair."

"Bim, I will say this to you once, and only once. Your days of bullying others to get what you want are OVER! From now on, you will do your own homework, you will stop being mean to other kids, and you will never ever, EVER mess with Marvin again! Do you understand me?"

"Yes," Bim squeaked back in a soft, high voice.

"I said, DO YOU UNDERSTAND ME?" as I pulled on Bim's hair even harder.

"Yes, yes, yes!" Bim cried out loudly. "I'm sorry, I'm sorry, please just let me go!"

I let Bim go and watched as his raisin-like scrunched-up face turned away. He grabbed the top of his head and started to run toward his house. As I put Marvin's money into my pocket, I noticed a big wet spot on the ground where Bim had been standing.

"How's that for a taste of your own medicine, Bim Bum?" I said. Bim kept running and never looked back. *Some "Average Joe" I am*, I thought to myself.

I started to walk back toward the school and then realized I'd better find out what time it was.

I reached into my backpack and pulled out my watch: 8:20. I had 25 minutes - plenty of time.

As soon as I got back to school, I walked into the building and headed straight for the bathroom.

AVERAGE JOE

Kids aren't allowed inside the school before the first bell rings at 8:55, but since I didn't look like a kid, I walked right by the office and nobody said a word.

I hung out in a bathroom stall until I had changed back into my 9-year old self. The first bell rang just as I was putting on my shoes. I shoved my dad's clothes and flip flops into my backpack and headed for class.

CHAPTER FOURTEEN
No More Worries

Marvin walked into class right after I had sat down. He looked depressed. His hair was messy, his t-shirt was on backwards, and he looked like he had just rolled out of bed.

"Guess what?" I said.

"What?" he said sadly.

I reached into my pocket and pulled out his money.

"I got your movie money back," I said.

Marvin's face lit up like a strobe light.

"How?" he asked.

"I told my Uncle Joe what Bim did to you, so he had a little talk with him. He told me that we don't have to worry about Bim anymore. Looks like you're going to the movie after all. I'll just give your money to Joe tonight."

"WOW! AWESOME!" Marvin said.

Just then Bim walked through the door. Marvin slumped down into his chair like he was trying to hide. Bim walked right by both of us and didn't say a word to anyone. He sat down in his seat and pulled out his math homework assignment and started working on it.

Marvin grabbed his math book and slid it into his desk.

"Don't worry Marvin," I said. "Bim's not going to take your homework from you anymore either."

Friday just seemed to fly by. It was a perfect day, except for the ton of homework that Miss Finkelstein gave us to do over the weekend.

Marvin was happier than I had ever seen before. All he could talk about was going to *Termination Experiment*.

Bim didn't say a word to anyone all day. He didn't look at anyone either. After lunch, Miss Finkelstein even sent Bim to the school nurse because she thought he was sick.

He's not sick, I thought to myself. *He's scared to death of my Uncle Joe - which means he's actually scared of me! How ironic!*

I was the last one to leave the classroom at the end of the day, and just as I got to the door, I heard Miss Finkelstein say, "Hey Joe, I met your uncle this morning."

"You did?" I said. "Where?"

"Out in front of the school while you were in the bathroom. He seems really nice."

You mean I seem really nice, I thought to myself.

"Yeah, he's pretty cool", I said. "It's fun having him live with us."

"Tell him I said, 'Hi,'" she said.

"Ok, I will," I said.

CHAPTER FIFTEEN
How Will He Know Us?

"Are you sure you can't go with us to the movie?" Marvin asked as we were walking home.

"I'm sure," I said. "I have to go to my other grandma's. Besides, I've already seen it. You and Jack are going to love it! It's one of the best movies I have EVER seen!

"I'll just tell Uncle Joe to meet both of you at the theater at ten minutes to one."

"How will he know us?" Marvin asked. "We've never met him."

"Well, he looks a lot like me, and I will show him yearbook pictures of both you and Jack tonight. I'm sure he'll be able to figure out who you are."

"I could just come by your house tonight and meet him," Marvin said.

"No, that won't work. He has to work until 11 p.m. Don't worry Marvin, he'll be there and he'll find you, I promise!"

"Will you tell him thanks for getting my money back for me?" Marvin asked.

"No, but you can do it yourself tomorrow," I said.

CHAPTER SIXTEEN
Another Close Call!

Saturday was finally here! Today was going to be the BEST DAY EVER! I couldn't wait to see *Termination Experiment*! I had my mom drop me off at the theatre at 12:40. I told her I wanted to get to the movie early so I could play video games in the lobby before the show with Jack and Marvin.

"Why are you taking your backpack to the movie?" my mom asked.

"Ummm, it's full of special *Slime Man* stuff," I said.

"Oh, OK," my mom said. "Make sure you bring all of your special *Slime Man* stuff back home with you."

Like I said before, my mom never looks in my backpack, and most of the time, that's a good thing!

"I'll just call you when I'm done," I said.

"No, we have to be to Grandma's by four, so I'll pick you up at 3:05 out front," she said.

Termination Experiment started at one and got out at 2:40. *If I take the Flawless Forever at 12:45, I'll have five minutes to ditch Jack and Marvin before I change back,* I thought. *That's plenty of time.*

I headed into the bathroom at the theater. I went into the corner stall, changed into my dad's clothes again, and swallowed a teaspoon of serum.

YAK, Uck, Yick, Bad, Bad, Bad! I'm certainly not getting used to the taste. In fact, I think it's getting worse!

I shoved my clothes and what was left of the Flawless Forever into my backpack and headed out the door to look for Jack and Marvin.

I spotted them right away. They were standing right in the middle of the lobby looking frantically for my "Uncle Joe."

"You must be Marvin and Jack," I said to them. "I'm Joe."

"Wow!" said Jack. "You look just like him!"

"Yeah, I get that a lot," I said.

"You even have a backpack like Joe's," Marvin said.

"Here's your money," Jack said.

"I gave my money to Joe yesterday," Marvin said.

"Yep, he already gave me your money, Marvin. Well, boys, let's buy our tickets," I said.

Getting into the movie was easy. Nobody suspected a thing. There I sat with my two best friends, watching the movie of my dreams. How could my life possibly get better?

Jack and Marvin talked to each other the whole time during the movie. They even shared a large popcorn, but they didn't ask me if I wanted some. At first, I felt left out, but then I realized, they don't even know my Uncle Joe, so why would they talk to him?

To me, *Termination Experiment* seemed to last forever. It wasn't at all what I expected it to be. In fact, it was kinda stupid. Jack and Marvin LOVED it! They said it was the best movie they had ever seen!

"I have to go now, boys," I told them as we were walking out of the theater. I have a test tomorrow and I need to study."

"Thanks for taking us, Joe," Jack said.

"Yeah, thanks!" said Marvin.

I started to head for the entrance to the mall. Just as I grabbed the door, I felt a tug on my shirt. I looked down. It was Marvin.

"Joe told me what you did for me, and he told me that you talked to Bim," Marvin said. "I just want to say thanks."

"Well, I did more than talk to Bim, Marvin, I scared the TEXAS out of him! If he ever bothers you again, just let Joe know."

"Thanks," said Marvin. "You're the BEST!"

I smiled back at Marvin and headed into the mall.

Two minutes - I had just two minutes to get out of sight before I changed back.

I found a broom closet next to the drinking fountain, and ducked into it just in time.

I changed back into me and headed straight for the video arcade. I had 15 minutes, ten bucks in my pocket and freedom to play any game that I wanted. I played *Box Car Blitz* for about ten minutes and then headed back to the theater mall exit.

Just as I walked outside, I saw Marvin and Jack getting into Jack's mom's van. My mom saw them too. Talk about a close call!

"I should have just had Jack's mom come and get you too, Joe, it would have made my day a lot easier. I wish I had thought about that and called her."

I'm so glad you didn't, I thought as we pulled out of the parking lot.

As soon as we got home from my grandma's that night, my mom made me clean my room - my closet included.

"You can't watch *Robotics International* with your dad until your room is spotless!" she said.

I decided to just keep the Flawless Forever in my backpack because as soon as I cleaned up my closet, I didn't have any dirty clothes to hide it in.

My original plan was to throw out what I didn't use, and put the jug back under the sink. But now, I was kind of getting used to the idea of having "Uncle Joe" around when I needed him.

CHAPTER 17
Karma

On Monday morning, just as I was about to set foot on the school grounds, I heard a gut-wrenching voice say, "Hey Joe, come over here." It was Bim!

The hair on the back of my neck stood straight up, I immediately started to sweat, and I got a rock-hard pain in my stomach.

What if Bim's scare had worn off? What if he was planning to beat me up just because Joe is my uncle? What if . . . ?

I walked over to Bim and stood still as he leaned over to talk to me.

AVERAGE JOE

"I was wondering if you could do me a favor?" Bim said in a nice, calm voice. "I was wondering if it would be okay if I rented your Uncle Joe."

"What?" I asked.

"I want to rent your Uncle Joe. I want him to scare my big brother Dax so he won't bully me anymore."

"Well," I said, "I don't think Joe. . ."

"I'll pay him 12 dollars," Bim said. "I'd pay even more if I had the money. Please, I am so sick of Dax. He makes my life miserable. I have to do his homework every night and now that Marvin isn't doing mine, I have to stay up until midnight to get everything done. If I don't do exactly what Dax says, he'll break my face."

That sounds familiar, I thought to myself.

"What do you want him to do?" I asked.

"Exactly what he did to me when I was picking on Marvin," he said.

"I guess I could ask him," I said. "You're not exactly his favorite person, but if I explain what's going on, he might agree to help. Can you give me the money now so I can show it to him? I don't think he trusts you very much either."

"Sure," Bim said. "Here it is."

He handed me a wad of cash, and then told me the route his brother takes on his way to the middle school.

"Here's a picture of him too so he will know what Dax looks like. I cut it out of his yearbook," he said. "He leaves our house at 7:15 a.m."

I looked at the picture…He looked exactly like Bim, only bigger. A lot bigger.

I tucked the money into my pocket.

"I'll see what I can do," I said.

Then I turned around and walked to class. *I'm glad I didn't dump out the Flawless Forever, I thought to myself. This Uncle Joe thing is really starting to pay off!*

CHAPTER EIGHTEEN
Love Note

Monday was a pretty uneventful day at school, other than Miss Finkelstein gave us extra credit homework to do on top of our regular four hours of homework. At my house, extra credit is called "required credit."

My mom always says, "Joe, your middle name is extra credit. Whenever it is offered, you have to do it because you never know when you're going to need it."

My four hours of homework just became five - ugh! I wish my parents would let me be average when it came to my grades.

I was the last one out of the classroom because I had to make sure that I had everything I needed to do my "required credit." Just as I was about to walk out the door, my teacher said, "Hey Joe, will you do me a favor? Give this note to your uncle for me."

She handed me a sealed envelope with "JOE" written in girlie letters on the outside.

"OK." I said. I threw the envelope into my backpack and ran out the door.

I was dying to find out what Miss Finkelstein had written in the note, but there was no way I could read it in front of Marvin and Jack. I'd have to wait until I got home, where I could be alone.

"Miss Finkelstein must not have a life," Marvin said. "She grades everything we hand in! It must take her hours every night."

"Who cares how long it takes her," I said. "It's me that I worry about."

"New teachers are totally like that," Jack said. "They totally come straight from college, where they learn to be Homework Ogres, and they totally forget what it's like to be a kid. Maybe we should secretly agree as a class to totally stop doing the homework. Then, maybe she'll totally realize what she's doing to us!"

AVERAGE JOE

Ever since we saw *Termination Experiment*, Jack has been using the word "totally" WAY TOO MUCH!

"Then she'll 'totally' fail everyone," I said.

"She can't fail everybody or she'll totally look bad," said Jack.

When I walked in through our back door into the kitchen, my mom was halfway inside the cupboard underneath the sink.

"Joe, have you seen the root beer jug that we got at the fair last year?"

Up went the hair on the back of my neck again.

"No," I said. "Why?"

"We are going to the fair as a family Friday night, and I am hoping that the root beer man will be there. If we can bring the jug we bought from him last year, he'll fill it up for half price. His root beer is the best that I have ever tasted! I thought I put the jug under the sink, but it isn't here. I must have put it someplace else," she said.

Before another lie came out of my mouth, I headed to my bedroom to read the note.

"Joe?" I heard Turtle say. "Want to hear my new accordion song? It's called the *Bellows Bop*."

"Turtle," I said, "I have a ton of homework to do."

"Please?" she said. "It's my new favorite song!"

On any other day, I would have told Turtle no, but then I thought about how mean Dax is to Bim, so I sat down in the chair and listened.

Bellows Bop sounded like *Bellows Bomb*! It was horrible. But to Turtle, it sounded like music! My little sister - a legend in her own mind!

"Want to hear my other song?" Turtle asked. "It's a waltz!"

"Not now Turtle, I have to do my homework," I said.

As soon as I got into my room, I locked the door behind me, reached into my backpack and pulled out the note.

Dear Joe –

It was great meeting you this week.
I really enjoy having your nephew in my class.
Maybe some time, we can get together for dinner.
Call me if you're interested.
Jane (453) 555-5555.

Holy Socks! I thought to myself. *Miss Finkelstein wants to date me!*

CHAPTER NINETEEN

Termination of the Homework Ogre

I tried to get most of my homework done before dinner, but I couldn't get my mind off the note. Just thinking about going on a date with Miss Finkelstein kinda grossed me out. In fact, the thought of dating, period, was gross.

My mom made tacos for dinner, my favorite. But when I sat up to the table, all I could think about was Miss Finkelstein. I guess she wasn't that bad looking for an old person.

"What's wrong Joe, are you sick? You haven't touched your dinner," my mom asked.

"No," I said, "just stressed about school."

"That teacher of yours gives way too much homework. Typical of a first year teacher," she said. "When she has kids of her own some day, she'll look back and realize how ridiculous her expectations are. Someone needs to talk to her and explain that kids have other obligations outside of school."

And then, I got another FANTASTIC IDEA! Maybe Uncle Joe can talk some sense into Miss Homework Ogre Finkelstein.

"Mom?" I asked. "Can I go to the fair with Marvin and Jack on Thursday?"

"We're going as a family on Friday," she said. "Besides, I don't think it's safe to go to the fair with just your friends."

"Can't I go twice?" I asked. "Marvin's parents can take us, and I'll spend my own money."

"Well," my mom said. "Turtle has her accordion lesson, and your dad has a late meeting scheduled at the lab, so I was thinking about letting you stay home alone anyway. But what if you have homework?"

"They aren't going until 5 p.m., so I can get most of it done before I leave and I'll finish after I get home. PLEASE? PLEASE?"

"Well, if you'll promise to start on your homework the minute you get home on Thursday, I guess that will be okay," she said.

I asked to be excused and ran to my bedroom. Then I ran back to the kitchen.

"Mom, I need an envelope for one of my homework assignments," I said.

My mom got up from the table and reached into the cupboard and pulled out a box of envelopes. She handed one to me.

"Here you go," she said.

I ran back to my bedroom and started to work on my newest homework assignment: "Termination of the Homework Ogre."

Since we have to write everything in cursive, Miss Finkelstein has never seen my printing, so "Uncle Joe" needed to print his reply to her note. I sat down at my desk and wrote:

Dear Jane –

It was great meeting you, too.

Would you like to go to the fair with me this Thursday? I have a big test on Friday, so I will need to go early, and I can't stay too late.

If this works for you, I can meet you at the front gate of the fairgrounds at 5 p.m. Just tell little Joe yes or no, and he will let me know.

I hope you can go.

Joe

I sealed the note inside the envelope, wrote "Jane" on the outside of it, and put it into my backpack. Then I worked on getting the rest of my homework done. By the time I finished it and got to bed, it was 10:30.

I couldn't sleep all night. I was too stressed out about dating my teacher, and scaring off Dax. I also felt bad about lying to my parents and my friends. Before I started taking Flawless Forever, I never lied to anyone. Now, it seems like all I do is lie to people.

CHAPTER TWENTY
Special Delivery

Tuesday morning, I stopped in at the office on my way to class, handed the "Jane" envelope to the secretary and asked her to put it in Miss Finkelstein's box. I told her it was from my uncle.

There was no way I was going to give a note like that to Miss Finkelstein personally. The last thing I needed right now was for a kid like Cody Annoying to think that I was trying to become a teacher's pet.

When I walked into my classroom, Miss Finkelstein seemed to go out of her way to be nice to me. All morning, she kept looking at me, smiling and nodding, like she expected me to tell her something. She gave me more attention this morning than she has given me this entire school year. It almost felt creepy.

While we were at lunch, she must have gone down to the office to check her mail box because when we came back into the classroom, I could tell she had read my note. Miss Finkelstein was wearing a smile that was as big as her entire face.

She was super nice to everyone this afternoon, even Cody Annoying. When the bell rang to go home, I started to head for the door.

"Joe," I heard Miss Finkelstein say to me. "Tell your uncle Joe YES. And tell him that teachers and their guests get free admission. He'll know what that means."

Her smiling face was bright red, and her eyes looked happier than I had ever seen them before. She looked like she had just won the lottery or something.

"OK, I will," I said.

Then I started to smile too. Uncle Joe to the rescue AGAIN!

CHAPTER TWENTY-ONE
Fashion Police Needed!

When I got home from school, Mom was on her way out the door with Turtle.

"I'm taking Turtle to her accordion lesson," my mom said. "I'll be back around five. Dad should be home by then too, so get a snack and get started on your homework."

"OK," I said.

As soon as the garage door started to close, I headed for my dad's closet. I had to pick out something for Uncle Joe to wear on his big date with Miss Finkelstein on Thursday night.

After rummaging through my dad's closet for about 15 minutes, I came to a concrete conclusion: My dad dresses like a total GEEK!

I managed to find a pair of khaki shorts with the tags still on them (way too un-geeky for my dad to wear), and an older faded polo (they never go out of style). I grabbed a belt, and a pair of underwear, and shoved everything into my backpack. On my way out of the room, I caught a glimpse of one of my dad's running shoes.

Shoes, I thought to myself. *What am I gonna do about shoes???*

I set my backpack down and pulled the closet door open again. There, tucked way in the back, was a brand-new pair of sandals with adjustable straps. They still had the tags on them too, and they were full of dust. PERFECT! I thought. *He'll never miss these.*

By the time my parents got home, I had most of my homework done. Miss Finkelstein was in such a good mood, that I think she forgot to give us our social studies homework.

"Hey Mom," I said. "I have to go early again for scenery team tomorrow."

"OK," she said. "What time do you need to leave?"

If Dax leaves his house for the middle school at 7:15, and my mom drops me off at the elementary at the same time, I'll have plenty of time to "run into him" along the way.

"7:10," I said. "I have to be there by 7:15."

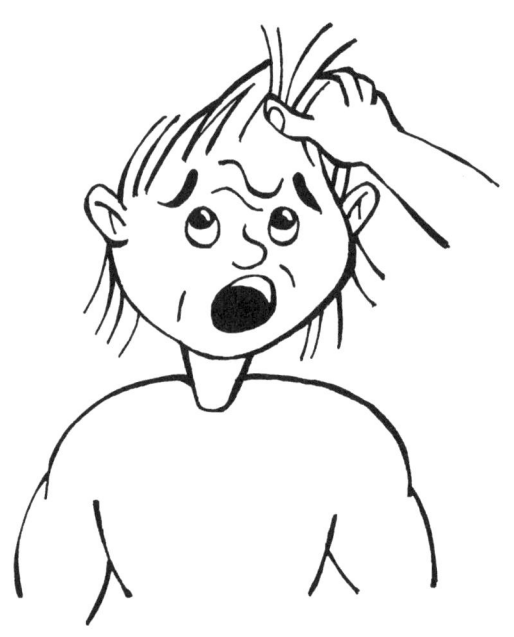

CHAPTER TWENTY-TWO
Bim on Steroids

My mom dropped me off in front of the school, right on time. I waved to her and hurried toward the front door. As soon as her car was out of sight, I ran across the street to the corner gas station and went inside the restroom.

I quickly changed into my date night clothes and took another dose of Flawless Forever. EEEWWWW!! BLAH!!! YUCK! YUCK! AAAHHH! *That stuff tastes SOOOOOOO BAD!* I thought.

I stood in front of the bathroom mirror thinking I could watch myself change, but when I blinked, I missed everything!

AVERAGE JOE

I gathered up my stuff and headed out to find Dax.

About five minutes later, I spotted a kid who could be Dax heading my way. He was big, and he looked a lot like Bim. Just as I opened my mouth to call out his name, I heard another kid say "Please Dax, don't."

I turned around and there he was - Dax! He was huge! He looked like Bim on steroids! He was holding a smaller kid's backpack by the strap and dangling it over the sewer, threatening to drop it in if the kid didn't pay him five dollars.

"Hey, Dax!" I yelled. "Come over here."

Dax looked up at me, smiled sarcastically, and then ignored me completely.

"Dax, you moron! Get over here now!" I screamed.

Dax looked up at me, threw the backpack at the face of its owner and started walking my way.

"What did you call me?" he said.

"A moron," I said, "because that's what you are!"

Dax reached out to grab my collar, but before he could reach me I grabbed him by the hair and threw him up against the fence. *Wow*, I thought. *Uncle Joe's strong!!*

"Who are you?" Dax asked in a shocked voice.

"It doesn't matter who I am. I need to talk to you about something," I said.

Inside my head, I was doing 400 jumping jacks per second, but on the outside, I amazingly managed to control myself again.

"Your little brother, Bim, told me that you make his life miserable every day."

"I have no idea what you are talking about," Dax said with a smirk on his face.

I held Dax up by his hair until he was standing on his tip toes.

"You are a bully, Dax! You push kids around. You make kids feel scared. You steal homework so you don't have to do it yourself. You even hurt own your little brother. You're a jerk!"

Dax's face turned as white as a sheet. His eyes got so big that I thought they were going to pop right out of his head.

"You have picked on Bim for the last time! From now on, you will be nice to him, and you will not threaten him in any way," I said as I pulled on his hair harder.

AVERAGE JOE

"OK, OK!" Dax said as he started to tremble. "Please, let go of my hair."

"Dax, I will say this to you once, and only once. Your days of bullying others to get what you want are OVER! From now on, you will do your own homework, you will stop being mean to other kids, and you will never ever, EVER mess with Bim again! Do you understand me?"

"Yes," Dax squeaked back in a soft, high voice.

"I said, DO YOU UNDERSTAND ME?" as I kept pulling harder on Dax's hair.

"Yes, yes, yes!" Dax cried out loudly. "I'm sorry, I'm sorry, please just let me go!"

I let Dax go and watched as his raisin-like scrunched-up face turned away. He grabbed the top of his head and started to run back toward his house. As I bent down to pick up my backpack, I noticed a big wet spot on the ground where Dax had been standing.

It must run in the family, I thought.

I walked back to the gas station and read magazines at the coffee counter until it was time for me to change back into myself. Luckily, the lady at the cash register was so busy that she didn't even notice when I went into the bathroom as a man and walked out as a boy.

*Not-So-Average Joe" strikes again!!!! –
Mission accomplished!*

CHAPTER TWENTY-THREE
Business as Usual

Today was business as usual at school.

Bim didn't say anything to me, but I bet he didn't know that I had "talked" to Dax.

Maybe Bim had already left for school when Dax came back home to change his clothes. If not, I'm sure that Dax would have avoided talking to Bim, considering his condition: bald and wet.

Miss Finkelstein realized that she forgot to give us our social studies homework yesterday, so to stay on schedule, she told us that we needed to do double homework tonight. The term "Homework Ogre" doesn't even come close to describing Miss Finkelstein lately.

"This has got to stop!" Marvin said. "I just can't take it anymore! I have my banjo lesson tonight and now I'll never get to bed! My doctor says that the only way I will start to grow is to get more sleep. At this rate, I'm going to be small enough to be a jockey!"

"Jockeys make a lot of money," said Jack.

"Yeah, but I can't ever be one," said Marvin. "I might end up being small enough, but I'm allergic to horses!"

"Maybe if we get all of our parents to go in and talk to Miss Finkelstein, she'll change," said Marvin."

"My parents won't do that," Jack said. "They love it that I have a lot of homework. They think it is preparing me for college."

"You're in the fourth grade," I said. "College is eons away!"

CHAPTER TWENTY-FOUR
It Worked!

This morning when I got to school, Bim came right over to me and gave me a high five.

"Thanks Joe!" he said. "Whatever your uncle told my brother must have worked because Dax hasn't picked on me now for two days."

"I'll tell him," I said. "Just remember what he told you."

Bim smiled at me and nodded. "I will," he said. Then he turned around and walked toward the front door.

AVERAGE JOE

When I walked into the classroom, I couldn't take my eyes off of Miss Finkelstein. She looked different! Her hair was curled, she was wearing makeup, and she even had that red goo stuff on her lips. She actually looked kinda cute for a teacher.

School went exactly as planned – lots of boring stuff that I had heard at least twice before, followed by lots of homework. Sometimes, I get so sick and tired of being in the fourth grade! I just feel so stuck!

I ran home after school as fast as I could. I wanted to get a good start on my homework before I took my teacher out on our first date. *Wow*, I thought to myself, *that just sounds so weird!*

CHAPTER TWENTY-FIVE
The BIG Date

I left for Marvin's house (actually the fairgrounds) at 4:30. Marvin has Karate tonight and his dad is out of town on a business trip, so I know his mom will be the one taking him. If for some reason my mom tries to call Marvin's house, no one will be at home. Marvin is my fantastic alibi and he doesn't even realize it.

I stopped in at the corner gas station again along the way, and did my bathroom transformation. I ended up having to run part of the way to get to the fairgrounds by five, but I made it just in time.

There she was waiting for me. My teacher- aka the Homework Ogre!

AVERAGE JOE

"Hi," I said. "You look nice!"

"Hi back," she said. "And so do you!"

Miss Finkelstein (or should I call her Jane?) used her free passes to get us through the gate.

We started walking toward the exhibits. She hauled me into the quilt building first, and spent 20 minutes (but it seemed like 20 hours) looking at blankets. I have never been more bored in my life!

"Hey," I said. "I have to leave by 6:40 to get to a study session at the college. Instead of looking at the exhibits, do you want to go on the rides?"

"Sure," she said, "but the gate passes we used don't let us go on the rides for free."

"That's okay," I said. "I'll pay our way."

We walked toward the midway. "Riding on the rides will be much more fun than looking at blankets, cows, and sheep," I said.

"Actually, I really enjoy the exhibits," Miss Finkelstein said. "But the rides are always fun too!"

I went to the ticket booth and bought two ride passes for 20 dollars. *It's a good thing Uncle Joe makes money!* I thought to myself.

We jumped on the Tilt-a-Whirl twice, rode the Ferris wheel once, and ended up riding the Zipper like ten times! I had a blast!

"Wow," she said to me, "you like these rides as much as my fourth graders do."

"How are your fourth graders anyway?" I asked.

"Actually, they're terrible! I am so frustrated with them! I give them homework every night and only about three kids in the class get it done and turn it in! Your nephew happens to be one of the good ones, by the way."

"How much homework do you give them?" I asked.

"Well, I need to give them something in every subject every night to strengthen their knowledge of what we cover during the day."

"That sounds like an awful lot of homework to me," I said. "They're only in fourth grade."

"I just want them to grow!" she said. "This class has so much potential! I just want to teach them everything I can!"

No, I thought to myself, *you just want to torture us.*

"You must spend a lot of time grading if the kids do that much homework," I said.

"Well, sometimes," she said.

"What about the kids who have scouts and music lessons and sports after school? When do they have time to do their homework?"

"School's the most important thing in a kid's life," she said. "A good education is the key to a bright future."

"I totally agree, but if you want kids to like school, you can't give them tons of homework every night. If a kid has to work hard all day in class, and then do hours of homework at night, they'll end up hating school. Kids need to have balance. They need time to play, and hang out with their friends too. Joe has more homework than I do some nights and I'm in college! I feel so sorry for him."

"Wow, I guess I never thought of it that way," Miss Finkelstein said. "I just want my students to be the best they can be in all that they do."

Then stop being a Homework Ogre, I thought.

"Well, then give them time to be kids and stop giving out so much homework," I said.

"You know, I think you're right," she said. "I probably should back off quite a bit. And, if I don't give out so much homework, I won't have to do so much grading at night too. I will say, I get pretty sick of it sometimes."

Just then, the alarm on my watch went off. "6:40," I said as I looked at my watch. "I have to go now, or I'll miss my study session. I'm sorry I have to leave."

"Oh, it's fine," she said. "I had a great time with you tonight. The rides were a lot of fun. I'll just stay here awhile and look at a few of the exhibits. I might even check out the cows and the sheep!"

She smiled at me and gave me a hug.

"Thanks for a fun time," I said.

Then I turned around and headed for the gate.

I hope I got through to her, I thought to myself as I started to run toward the gas station. *I hope the Ogre has been terminated.*

CHAPTER TWENTY-SIX
Not-So-Average Joe after All!

I slept right through my alarm this morning. I must have been really tired. I was so late getting to school that my mom had to drive me.

When I walked into my classroom, Miss Finkelstein said, "Hi," and then flashed me a smile. I seriously think that now because of "Uncle Joe," I am becoming the teacher's pet.

As soon as the bell rang, Miss Finkelstein made a statement that shocked everyone - including me.

"Class, I need to apologize to all of you," she said.

"I've been giving you way too much homework this year and I realize now that you need more free time to do the things that kids do. From now on, we will only have homework in one subject each night. Also, the most I want you to spend on your homework is 30 minutes, so I'm going to make your homework assignments shorter. You will still have to study your spelling words every night, but I think this new system will be a lot better for everyone."

The kids all stared at Miss Finkelstein with their mouths wide open. They couldn't believe what they were hearing.

Oh my gosh! It worked! I thought to myself. *Not-So-Average Joe did it again! The Homework Ogre has been terminated!*

The rest of my day at school went by really fast. After lunch, the drama teacher passed around a sign-up sheet for kids who wanted to help design the sets for the school play. I made sure I signed up.

Jack, Marvin and I celebrated the whole way home! "The Homework Ogre is no more - she's been TERMINATED that's for sure!" we chanted over and over again.

"Did your mom totally call the principal on Miss Finkelstein and totally complain about how much homework we've be getting?" Jack asked me on the way home from school.

"No," I said. "Hey Marvin, did your mom call?"

"She might have called, but I didn't see her do it," he said.

"Someone must have totally called and complained," said Jack. "And now my life is totally awesome!!"

When I got home, my dad's car was in the driveway. He must have gotten off early today.

When I walked inside the house, my dad was standing in the kitchen holding some Flawless Forever in one hand, and a test tube full of blue stuff in the other.

"Joe," he said, "I've got it! I've figured out the perfect switch back serum! I think it will really work this time! Follow me down to the lab so I can hook you up to the monitors. I want to try this out on you right away."

I started to feel sick inside.

"OK," I said, "but I need to use the bathroom first."

I closed the bathroom door behind me just as my dad headed downstairs.

Wow, I thought to myself. *I'm really liking having Uncle Joe around. I'm not so sure I want things to go* back to being the way they used to be. *If my dad's new switch back serum works, I'll be just like everyone else again. I'll just be average.*

I looked into the mirror and stared at my face. *I do hate having to lie to people all the time, though.* I thought.

I slowly reached into my backpack and grabbed my jug of Flawless Forever. I carefully opened up the jug, poured what was left into the bathroom sink and watched as it disappeared down the drain. I rinsed out the bottle, and put it back under the kitchen sink behind the paper towels. Then, I headed downstairs to the lab.